DATE DUE

OCT 2 1 2000			
DEC 0 1 2000			
DEC 1 5 2000			
MAR 1 9 2001			
APR 1 2 2001			
GAYLORD			PRINTED IN U.S.A.

A Note About the Illustrations

The person we know as Santa Claus in America and Britain originated in Europe, where his appearance in various countries varies according to religious traditions.

The illustrator of this story, Jean-Pierre Corderoc'h, is Catholic and lives in a part of France where the kind man who distributes gifts during the Christmas season is called Saint Nicholas. According to legend, Nicholas was a wealthy man, known for his love of children and his acts of generosity to people less fortunate than himself. He became a bishop in the early Christian church, at Myra, in what is now Turkey. In parts of France and in the German-speaking countries of Europe, Saint Nicholas is still depicted as the Bishop of Myra—grand and stately in his Episcopal robes.

Although they may look different from each other, the European Saint Nicholas and our Santa Claus have the same gentle, loving spirit and devotion to children.

Copyright © 1992 by Nord-Süd Verlag AG, Gossau Zürich, Switzerland
First published in Switzerland under the title *Kann ich dir helfen, Nikolaus?*
English translation copyright © 1992 by Rosemary Lanning.

First published in the United States, Great Britain, Canada,
Australia, and New Zealand in 1992 by North-South Books,
an imprint of Nord-Süd Verlag AG, Gossau Zürich, Switzerland.
First paperback edition published in 1998.

Distributed in the United States by North-South Books Inc., New York.

Library of Congress Cataloging-in-Publication Data
Scheidl, Gerda Marie.
(Kann ich dir helfen, Nikolaus? English)
Can we help you, Saint Nicholas? / Gerda Maria Scheidl;
illustrated by Jean-Pierre Corderoc'h; translated by Rosemary Lanning.
Summary: When Saint Nicholas oversleeps on Christmas Eve,
the forest animals find ways to help him so he won't
disappoint the village children.
1. Santa Claus—Juvenile fiction.
(1. Santa Claus - Fiction. 2. Christmas - Fiction.
3. Forest animals - Fiction.)
I. Corderoc'h, Jean-Pierre, ill. II. Title
PZ7.S3429Can 1992
(E) - dc20 92-5231

A CIP catalogue record for this book is available from The British Library.

ISBN 1-55858-956-2 (paperback)
1 3 5 7 9 PB 10 8 6 4 2
Printed in Belgium

For more information about our books, and the authors and artists
who create them, visit our web site: http://www.northsouth.com

Gerda Marie Scheidl

Can We Help You, Saint Nicholas?

ILLUSTRATED BY
Jean-Pierre Corderoc'h

TRANSLATED BY
Rosemary Lanning

North-South Books
NEW YORK · LONDON

It was Christmas Eve, the busiest day of his year, and Saint Nicholas had overslept. He was so angry with himself that he rushed out in far too much of a hurry and lost his way.

"I'm getting old," sighed Saint Nicholas. "First I oversleep, then I lose my way. How am I going to find the children now?"

He rubbed his eyes. "If only it were not so dark," he thought. Then he called out: "Are you there, moon? Could you light the way for me?"

Saint Nicholas waited impatiently, but the moon didn't appear. It was hiding behind a cloud and wouldn't come out.

"Can I help you, Saint Nicholas?" asked an owl, perched above him in a tree.

"I wish you could," said Saint Nicholas. "But I can't imagine how."

"I can."

"Really?" said Saint Nicholas, doubtfully.

The owl nodded. "I can see in the dark." He fluffed up his feathers importantly. "I'll show you the way. Just follow me. *Tu-whit, tu-whoo.*" The owl spread his wings wide and flew off.

Saint Nicholas hesitated, but only for a moment, then followed the owl into the night.

At last the moon came out from behind its cloud. Saint Nicholas trudged after the owl, trying to keep up with him, but after a while he stopped.

The owl looked back. "Are you tired?" he asked anxiously.

"No, not tired," said Saint Nicholas. "I'm hungry. I forgot to eat my toast and honey."

"Shall I fetch you a mouse to eat?"

"Ugh!" Saint Nicholas shuddered. "I don't eat mice!"

"I do!" hooted the owl, glaring at a little mouse who was hopping inquisitively towards them.

"No! Leave her alone!" cried Saint Nicholas, shooing the owl away.

The little mouse had only seen Saint Nicholas, not the owl. She sat down on a tree trunk, looked at him and said…

"Can I help you, Saint Nicholas?"

Saint Nicholas smiled. "You? I don't think so. I'm hungry."

In an instant the mouse had disappeared under a hazel bush. She came back with three hazelnuts which she rolled up to Saint Nicholas's feet.

"There you are," piped the little creature.

"Thank you," said Saint Nicholas. He picked up the three nuts, but now he had another problem—how was he to crack them?

   "Can I help you, Saint Nicholas?" asked a squirrel, leaping
through the pine trees.
   "Yes," said Saint Nicholas. "You can crack these nuts for me."
   The squirrel cracked the nuts in no time. Saint Nicholas
thanked her, and ate them hungrily, enjoying every mouthful.
   "Have you had enough to eat?" asked the mouse.
   "Indeed I have," said Saint Nicholas with a smile.
   "Then it's time we went on," said the owl.
   "May I come with you?" asked the squirrel.
   "If you like," said Saint Nicholas.

"I want to come too," squeaked the little mouse.

"You?" said the owl, bobbing and blinking crossly at her.

"Now, now," said Saint Nicholas. "You can *all* come if you promise to be nice to each other." The squirrel and the mouse promised, though the little mouse crept closer to Saint Nicholas for safety.

"And what about you, owl? Do you promise?" said Saint Nicholas, looking solemnly at the owl.

The owl looked uncomfortable, but he couldn't disappoint
Saint Nicholas. "I promise," he said gruffly. Then he spread his
wings and flew deeper into the woods.

Saint Nicholas followed him. The squirrel leapt from tree
to tree and the little mouse pattered along behind. The mouse
wasn't used to running in the cold snow. Normally she would
have been asleep at this time of year.

"I could carry the mouse in my beak," suggested the owl craftily. "Then her little feet wouldn't get so cold."

"Oh no," squeaked the mouse. "That would be much too dangerous. I'd rather go this way." She hopped onto Saint Nicholas's cloak and allowed herself to be pulled across the snow, squeaking happily as she bounced along.

Suddenly the wind began to whistle through the treetops. Saint Nicholas huddled behind a rock, but it didn't give him much shelter.

"Achoo!" went Saint Nicholas.

"Can I help you, Saint Nicholas?" asked a bear, who had crawled out of his cave.

"I don't think so," said Saint Nicholas, shivering violently.

"Come into my warm cave," said the bear. "You'll get sick if you stay outside."

"I can't," said Saint Nicholas. "There isn't time. The children are waiting for me…"

"But if you get sick, the children will wait even longer."

"You're right, and that would be terrible." Saint Nicholas climbed into the cave, and the squirrel and the mouse and the owl followed.

The bear's cave was warm and cozy, and they all snuggled close to the bear. No one was cold anymore.

At last the wind stopped howling and everything was quiet. "Now we can go on," said Saint Nicholas with relief. They all went with him—even the bear.

Saint Nicholas strode ahead. Soon they came to the edge of the forest and saw lights twinkling in the valley below.

Saint Nicholas was about to say, "At last!" when he tumbled into the snow. The bear disappeared too, along with the squirrel and the mouse. The owl fell out of his tree in surprise.

There was a hole under the snow and they had all fallen in. Only the tip of Saint Nicholas's hat, one of the bear's ears and the owl's wing could be seen. Surely no one could help them now.

Luckily a passing reindeer saw them fall. With his powerful antlers he dug Saint Nicholas, the bear, the squirrel and the owl out of the snow. But there was no sign of the mouse.

"Have you eaten the mouse?" said Saint Nicholas sternly to the owl.

"How could you think that?" said the owl, ruffling his feathers indignantly. "I keep my promises."

The bear sniffed Saint Nicholas's sack. Saint Nicholas opened it and everyone looked inside.

There sat the mouse, nibbling a little ginger cake. "Tut, tut," said Saint Nicholas. "You mustn't nibble the things in my sack. They are all for the children."

The mouse looked rather ashamed of herself.

"On we go," said Saint Nicholas, closing his sack.

A steep slope led down to the village where the children were waiting for their presents.

"I'm so tired," said Saint Nicholas despairingly. "I'll *never* get down there."

"Climb on my back," said the reindeer, "I'll carry you."

Saint Nicholas climbed onto the reindeer, and as they galloped down to the village he cried, "Goodbye, my friends. I can't thank you enough!"

The animals sat quietly and watched as Saint Nicholas disappeared. "Goodbye!" they yelled back. "We'll be here again next year if you need help!"